SCUBA DIVER

WILD JOBS

LAURA K. MURRAY

CREATIVE EDUCATION · CREATIVE PAPERBACKS

PUBLISHED BY CREATIVE EDUCATION AND CREATIVE PAPERBACKS
P.O. Box 227, Mankato, Minnesota 56002
Creative Education and Creative Paperbacks are
imprints of The Creative Company
www.thecreativecompany.us

DESIGN AND PRODUCTION by Joe Kahnke
Art direction by Rita Marshall
Printed in the United States of America

PHOTOGRAPHS by Alamy (13UG 13th, Mark Conlin, Paul Ives,
Emmanuel LATTES, PJF Military Collection, WaterFrame, ZUMA Press,
Inc.), Getty Images (Giordano Cipriani, Sameh Wassef), LostandTaken.
com, National Geographic Creative (JAD DAVENPORT, MAURICIO
HANDLER, NORBERT WU/MINDEN PICTURES), Shutterstock
(fenkieandreas, Husjak, Hoiseung Jung, Kletr, J. S. Lamy, Lizard, Betti
Luna, Nik Merkulov, Miloje, peiyang, Egor Shilov, Sergiy Zavgorodny)

Library of Congress Cataloging-in-Publication Data
Names: Murray, Laura K., author.
Title: Scuba diver / Laura K. Murray.
Series: Wild Jobs.
Includes bibliographical references and index.
Summary: A brief exploration of what scuba divers do on the job, including
the equipment they use and the training they need, plus real-life instances
of scuba diving to discover ancient, underwater cities.
Identifiers: ISBN 978-1-60818-925-0 (hardcover) / ISBN 978-1-62832-
541-6 (pbk) / ISBN 978-1-56660-977-7 (eBook)
This title has been submitted for CIP processing under LCCN 2017940124.

CCSS: RI.1.1, 2, 3, 4, 5, 6, 7; RI.2.1, 2, 4, 5, 6; RI.3.1, 2, 5, 7; RF.1.1, 3, 4; RF.2.3, 4

FIRST EDITION HC 9 8 7 6 5 4 3 2 1
FIRST EDITION PBK 9 8 7 6 5 4 3 2 1

CONTENTS

SUNLIGHT BEAMS INTO THE WATER.

You kick your fins and dive deeper. The water gets colder. Suddenly, a stingray glides by. You record it with your underwater camera.

1
WILD WORK

Scuba divers have many underwater jobs. Some are scientists. They study the underwater world. Other divers have military or public safety jobs. They rescue people. They even help with solving crimes.

Scuba divers may work in construction, repair, and drilling. Others do **SURVEYS** and mapping. They search for sunken cities and wrecks.

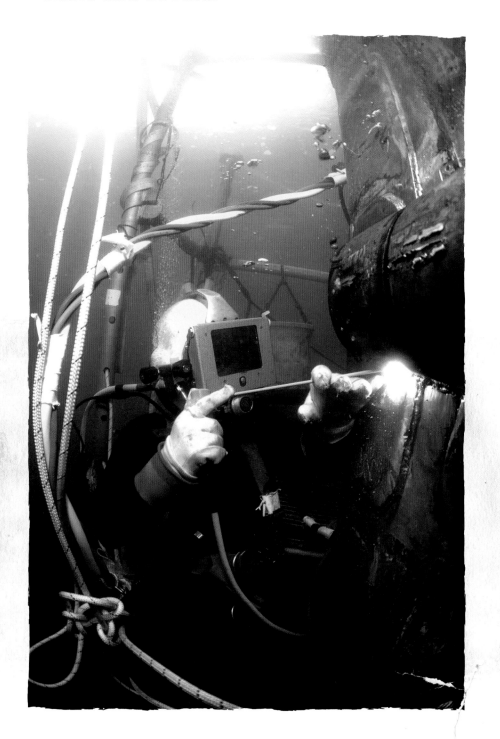

2 EQUIPPED TO DIVE

Scuba divers explore oceans, lakes, and rivers. Skilled divers go beyond 130 feet (39.6 m) deep. They dive among sharks, coral reefs, and other wild things.

Divers make sure their equipment works properly.
They must not dive or surface too quickly.
Otherwise, they may hurt their lungs or get sick.

3 TRAINING FOR SAFETY

Scuba divers need special training. Different jobs require **CERTIFICATIONS**, too. The divers learn to stay safe and communicate underwater. They learn **CPR** and first aid.

Scuba divers wear a wetsuit or a drysuit. These keep them warm. They have a mask, fins, and gloves. They need a tank and **REGULATOR** to breathe. Divers carry a watch, **COMPASS**, gear bag, and lights.

4 UNDERWATER CITY

In 1967, **OCEANOGRAPHER** Nicholas Flemming was diving near Greece. There he discovered the underwater city of Pavlopetri. It could be around 5,000 years old! Divers still study the city today.

5
IS DIVING FOR YOU?

Scuba divers have many underwater adventures. Would *you* want to be a scuba diver when you grow up?

YOU BE THE SCUBA DIVER!

Imagine you are a scuba diver. Read the questions below about your wild job. Then write your answers on a separate sheet of paper. Draw a picture of yourself as a scuba diver!

My name is _____. I am a scuba diver.

1. What jobs do you perform?
2. What types of animals do you see?
3. How does the water feel?
4. What skills do you need?
5. How do you stay safe underwater?

GLOSSARY

CERTIFICATIONS: proofs of certain skills

COMPASS: an object used to show direction

CPR (CARDIOPULMONARY RESUSCITATION): a life-saving act to make someone's heart and lungs work again

OCEANOGRAPHER: a scientist who studies the ocean

REGULATOR: an object that controls pressure

SURVEYS: examinations of an area to record its features

READ MORE

Greve, Tom. *Scuba Diving*.
Vero Beach, Fla.: Rourke, 2009.

Uttridge, Sarah, ed. *Ocean Animals around the World*.
Mankato, Minn.: Smart Apple Media, 2015.

WEBSITES

The Ocean
https://www.nwf.org/Kids/Ranger-Rick/Animals/Mixture-of-Species/Ocean-Animals.aspx
Read all about the ocean and its animals.

Ocean Portal
http://kids.nationalgeographic.com/explore/ocean-portal/
Explore ocean life through games and videos.

Note: Every effort has been made to ensure that the websites listed above are suitable for children, that they have educational value, and that they contain no inappropriate material. However, because of the nature of the Internet, it is impossible to guarantee that these sites will remain active indefinitely or that their contents will not be altered.

INDEX